AWAKENING CROW MOON

AND OTHER POEMS AND SHORT STORIES

A Wild and Wonderful Experience in the Poetry of Life

SHIRLEY HEDRICK WILLIAMS

Copyright © 2020
Shirley Hedrick Williams
FIRE and GRACE Publishing, LLC
Awakening Crow Moon
And Other Poems And Short Stories
A Wild and Wonderful Experience in the Poetry of Life
All rights reserved.

No part of this publication may be reproduced, distributed, or transmitted in any form or by any means, including photocopying, recording, or other electronic or mechanical methods, without the prior written permission of the publisher, except in the case of brief quotations embodied in critical reviews and certain other non-commercial uses permitted by copyright law.

Shirley Hedrick Williams
FIRE and GRACE Publishing, LLC
fireandgracepublishing.com

Printed in the United States of America
First Printing 2020
First Edition 2020

ISBN: 978-1-7349381-1-1

10 9 8 7 6 5 4 3 2 1

The short stories are works of fiction. Names, characters, places, and incidents are the products of the author's imagination or are used fictitiously. Any resemblance to actual events, locales, or persons, living or dead, is entirely coincidental.

Cover Design by VC Book Cover Design

To my son, Terrence Hedrick Williams, who urged me to compile my poetry into a book
and
To my daughter, Melissa Plantz, who encouraged me through every step of this journey, and made it happen.
Thank you both.
I love you dearly.

Table of Contents

PART I 1

A Wild And Wonderful Experience In The Poetry Of Life

LOVE SONNET TO THE LAND 2
AWAKENING CROW MOON 3
THE LAND OF THE EVERGREEN GROVE 4
THE SEARCH 5
WHERE BRIGHT WATERS DASH 6
NATURE'S HAUNTING TUNE 7
GOLDEN FLIGHT 8
WHEN I KNEEL 9
SEEKING SOLACE 10
TRANSITION 11
THIS HURT 12
HAVE A LITTLE FAITH 13
THE STONES CRY OUT! 14
PICNIC IN THE MORNING SUN 15
FENCES ARE MADE TO CLIMB 16
WAYWARD WIND 17
A CHAPEL 18
QUIET TIME 19
PRECIOUS GEMS 20
SHARP CHIRPS OF SWEET SPRING 21
DEAR MEMORY SINGS 22
ANCIENT SECRETS OF A MYSTIC COUNTRYSIDE 23

FRAGMENTS OF FAITH 25

JEWELED MOMENTS 26

GOODBYE 27

TO SUMMON 28

WAYS AND ROADS 29

WHEN WIND BEGINS TO WHIP 30

MY HEART RECALLS 31

BONN'S BEETHOVEN BOY 32

IF THIS BE CHRIST CRUCIFIED (WHAT THE SHROUD MEANS TO ME) 33

ON HEARING HANDEL'S MESSIAH 36

PART II 37

Short Stories From The Hills Of West Virginia

WELCOME HOME 38

THE DISAPPEARANCE OF FANNY BARBERTON 50

SOUL STALKER 56

ABOUT THE POET AND AUTHOR 73

PART I

*A Wild And Wonderful Experience
In The Poetry Of Life*

LOVE SONNET TO THE LAND

Now I return to my beloved home state

Where bracing mountain air will lift my head;

Where heights will raise my hopes and make faith great,

And leafy wilderness will form my bed;

Where I may find the peace sweet bowers bring,

Rejoice in spirit as I wade cool streams;

Where I can hear the whippoorwill still sing,

And know the wonder of deep woodland dreams—

Where I glimpse him, though he is gone from me

Into bright regions of a realm too vast

For eyes to follow close enough to see

But resurrecting grace of God that lasts.

This is my heart's love sonnet to the earth

That gave it life and, giving, gave me worth.

AWAKENING CROW MOON

It is the time of the awakening crow moon,

The vernal equinox of my life.

A time for eating wintercress;

A time for dandelions and chickweed,

For riding clouds when they run

Or caressing sunshine when it comes.

I look for violets to sweeten perspective-

Finding, for looking, trailing arbutus

To scent the circumference of my soul.

A blood-dipped maple has to shelter me

Until this unpredictability shall pass, I know,

But for now I am content

To watch the winds carry my thoughts

Catching my words on the crow moon.

THE LAND OF THE EVERGREEN GROVE

The land of the evergreen grove

Lies silent with carpets of snow,

Rabbit tracks enticing eyes

To follow life into clear contrasts

Of shadow and light.

I stand alone in reverent peace

Encircled by a ring of evergreens,

Like bejeweled fur-frocked worshippers,

Watching the Morning Star arise

Atop a tree transformed

With fine latticework of white.

Quietly, the birds begin to sing

As day dawns within me too,

And I see Nature's

Celebrated Christmastide.

THE SEARCH

I searched for God in great evergreens of earth
Holding deeply scented mysteries in sight,
While warm living branches like giant wreaths
Adorn a forlorn world in weary calendar days
I almost touched the hem of His robe.
I searched for God in towering cathedral spires-
Their foundations reverent with rich adoration-
Pointing toward always changing skies of white clouds
Scuttling through blue streams,
Or gray rolls of river rain.
I almost caught His smile of recognition.
I searched for God in brilliant stars-
Their bright glory blazing a path through space-
Until nearly blind.
I almost saw His eyes.
I searched for God in the Book of books
Which brought me closer to the truth of trust.
I almost fathomed the mind of the Son of Man.
Then tired but hungry and hopeful,
I bowed my head before an unseen Lord
And saw within my heart His face.

WHERE BRIGHT WATERS DASH

I follow Gauley where bright waters dash

Around big boulders in a dizzy swirl,

Before white waves spring back to leap and crash

Cascading quickly over rocks and hurl

Themselves into the rushing river bed;

And always all around the mountains stand

Tall trees in Summer's branching green well fed,

Or kingly colors when Fall crowns the land,

Or winter's snowcaps rising as I wait

In dreams of blue and gold adorning face,

And hint that coming Spring will quicken gait—

Release the river to the current's race.

If Earth be shadows of the things to come,

I'll search for Gauley when I pass the sun.

NATURE'S HAUNTING TUNE

He is all that man desires,

Joy this life contains,

Love to which the heart aspires,

Peace the mind retains.

He is music ears have heard,

Nature's haunting tune,

Song of dawn or soaring bird

Under mellow moon,

Hue and shadow eyes admire

At the break of day,

And the glow of sunset's fire

Warming souls who pray.

Some call Him the law of space-

Worlds in one accord-

I call Him the Saving Grace,

Jesus Christ and Lord.

GOLDEN FLIGHT

A butterfly took his last golden flight
Still touching flower petals as he fell,
Though only God kept him in perfect sight
Bade Black-Eyed Susan final soft farewell,
Then fluttered to my feet and clutched the grass
In such triumphant manner I too felt
The feather-tap of wing (and could not pass
Without respectful pause lest heart bear guilt.)
O Life transformed through timely spun cocoon
From lowly worm to caterpillar dream
Accomplished, finished, plan complete so soon!
I hold your brilliant goal in high esteem.
Some may mistake that form for fallen leaf-
My eyes see beauty soar however brief.

WHEN I KNEEL

Sometimes I feel too discouraged.
Sometimes I feel downright blue.
When I kneel before You Father
You always lift me to You.

You give me courage when I falter.
You give peace when I am stressed.
You give me hope to face the future,
And in Your love I am blessed.

Thank You, Father, for Your sweet presence.
Thank You, Lord, for everything.
Thank You, dear Savior, For Your mercy-
Jesus Christ the soon coming King.

SEEKING SOLACE

I walk through sorrow's damp, dark wood;

A large cloud threatens rain.

Fall trees give solace for my food;

I search more, but in vain.

Then catch a glimpse of shining Son,

See flowers circle stones.

Hope sings; and I begin to run

To hear her long, lost tones!

TRANSITION

Why does the ice resist the sun's warm ray?

To prove that hearts remain forever cold,

Though warm and sweet but only yesterday?

Love's salutation once so dear if old

Has passed the hardness of reality

Revealed in every step I dare to take

On silent planets of eternity,

The word *forever* keeping mind awake

When heart would rather yield in melting grief;

To find the soothing softness of relief;

To know again all tragedies *do* end.

It is not time alone which softens ice,

But all intensive warmth melts cold's device.

THIS HURT

What shall I do with this hurt?

Weep over Jerusalem

Under the blue moon of the night

Adorn this pain with flowers and palms

In sunshine until it withers

With too much heat?

Or cover it with warm rich earth

Where life can bloom above?

Or suspend it indefinitely

 As webs woven by deceptive minds,

Or as icicles formed from hardened hearts?

Innocence seeks the silent dark

To suffer alone, yet never dies.

Innocence sings on in the sun

Solely to please the pure in thought.

Roll

    The

        Stone

            Away

HAVE A LITTLE FAITH

"Have a little faith,"
Mother used to say.
"Have a little faith.
God will make a way."

"Have a little faith."
And so I believed
It would all work out,
And my mind relieved.

Now that she is gone,
I still hear her pray.
Have a little faith.
God will make a way.

THE STONES CRY OUT!

If men kept quiet touching Jesus' life,

The very stones would cry aloud He said.

Except the blast and bomb of yearly strife

My world stood silent, empty, lost and dead

Until a multi-colored morning sky

Conveyed new music through the air to me—

Mechanical voices pictured on high

Extoling Christ, His Love, His Sovereignty;

The message says He comes to raise

A fellowship reborn to pure perfection.

Ten-thousand tongues dare sing His praise

And crystal rocks resound the Resurrection!

PICNIC IN THE MORNING SUN

Dancing rings on sunlit streams-
in subliminal cut manner-
reflect first one passing form
(human leg, puppy paw, feather then another).
Tinting my little girl's long brown hair
With streaks of sun-spun gold,
Life glistens as she listens
To pastoral lines by our local poet.
Sunlight filters through shelter of leaves
Delicately gilding long thick lashes
Of a blue-eyed friend deeply drawn
Into his contemplative conversation.
A glossy sheen on the coat of a collie,
And a bright amber gleam
From the fur of a red-bone hound
Vie for the eye of our snap-shot photographer.
I sit, a Monet without his skill or paint,
High in silent sighs of light and shade
Impressing my brain to remember.

FENCES ARE MADE TO CLIMB

For now, my baby boy,

You sleep safely in your mesh playpen.

You lie dreaming securely on your stomach,

Your white neck defenseless to the world,

Your curly head resting trustingly upon the soft mat.

Rightly so – Mother watches over you,

Knowing full well there will come a time

You will think fences are made to climb.

Your pioneer spirit,

Your explorer's indomitable mind

Will soon question barriers to your goals.

Warning of drugs and thugs,

Mother will cling to one last fragile hold

Until you snap the string

To walk away a man well warned.

For now you sleep safely in your mesh playpen

Never dreaming fences are made to climb.

WAYWARD WIND

Brushing leaves aside,

The wayward wind of West Virginia

Sweeps through tree branches and reveals

An old Mill still standing at the end

Of a road in Greenbrier County.

I walk through wooded hollows

Hiding eighteenth century secrets and imagine

The mill moving, working steadily

Before it ground to a stop.

Because I cannot stay to gaze

Into the leaf framed windows,

There is a likeness in the wind and me.

But in my mind lives this haunting scene:

An old log mill standing in the woods-

That and the wayward wind.

A CHAPEL

A chapel built upon a solid Rock

Stands guard within my spirit's fort.

My heart beats faster as the dark storms knock

These outer walls of fleshly court.

Still, there – unchanged by any foes –

The Light upon the altar glows.

QUIET TIME

She paints

Rose-ribboned peace

Soft mantle on her mind

In mellow shades of summer

Sunset.

PRECIOUS GEMS

Daybreak forms bright silver links

Grasses glisten fiery blue,

Turn to sparkle sapphire pinks

Catching falling crystal dew.

Artists reach for precious hue

Ephemeral dawning rays display!

O God of light!

O God of might!

Nothing is too hard for you!

SHARP CHIRPS OF SWEET SPRING

Sharp chirps of sweet spring

All winging on damp breezes

A cosmos in song.

DEAR MEMORY SINGS

Dear memory sings

Through space alive with movement

My reverie's ghost.

ANCIENT SECRETS OF A MYSTIC COUNTRYSIDE

Come climb with me into the West Virginia woods.
There I will show you Golden paths and wine-red trails
Which winding through these dense, huge forests soon unveil
Their shapes and forms by casting off their Autumn hoods.
It is Fall on the West Virginia peaks
When driving free from city fumes and leaks
Or on from chunks of Coal to Sandstone, fossilized shale,
I know a knoll where quilts of scarlet leaves will hide
The ancient secrets of a mystic countryside.

The waterfalls freeze in degrees of sinking lows.
Unbridled wind in West Virginia blows crust-cold,
But cliffs that grasp one-sided spruce have grown quite old
While waiting out the soundless season of white snow.
It is cold in the West Virginia hush
When driving free from dreaded dirty slush,
Or through the traffic jam to underground ice flow.
I know a place where quiet echoes through the land,
Where footprints glisten in renewed yet recalled sand.

Unrestricted streams cascade over settled rock
Where Rhododendron and cross-crowned dogwood bloom.
I wander through the long-gone sea's chilled caverned rooms,

Or hike mountains with my homemade alpenstock.
It is Spring in the West Virginia field-
So driving free from work I then must yield,
Turn back from highrise structures to foliaged heirlooms.
I know solid Seneca, windblown Dolly Sod,
Artistic creations of our Almighty God.

Soft silken waters slip through undergrowth of trees,
If I sit silent, breathless in the cool, green shade
Of maple leaves before this day begins to fade,
I hear the distant droning of the meadow bees.
It is June in the West Virginia hills.
When driving free from industrial spills
Or passing coal mines to West Virginia's arctic glade,
I know a river whose clear water glides smooth stones –
Whose secrets make think of prehistoric bones.
On levels high with mountain laurel or low with Goldenrod,
There lies this rugged land brushed by a touch of the hand of God.

FRAGMENTS OF FAITH

Fragments of Faith

Fallen at my feet

Sharp points of pain

Piercing my heart

Shattered pieces

Reflecting the face of God

I offer slivers of faith

To Him in prayer.

Reaching into the depths of soul

He restores faith and makes me whole.

JEWELED MOMENTS

There gleams a young elm

With slender, rain-drenched branches.

Its worth, a bronze leaf.

There shines an old oak

With many mighty branches.

Bare limbs set with sun.

A royal blue dome,

My monumental mountain,

And my Autumn-gold crown.

GOODBYE

Her hands

Touched tinkling glass,

Her fingers, painted hearts,

The windchimed words of a last love

Letter.

TO SUMMON

No word in all the world can call you here.

No line of thought or form can bring you back.

No touch, embrace or kiss can keep you near

When life must leave the well-known human track

To wind the dark enchantment of deep death.

Perceiving Plato's all perceiving mind,

Or learning by impeded burning breath

Young Aristotle's great eternal find.

A search for wisdom in the books of old,

A love for labor and the food you crave,

A value priced far higher than our gold,

All over for the happy mental-slave.

Yet I will live to summon all my art,

Evoke your image in my loving heart.

WAYS AND ROADS

Strolling summer roads with you near

Is one way of saying hello.

Walking from your grave without fear

Is a way of letting you go.

WHEN WIND BEGINS TO WHIP

When wind begins to whip sustaining stem,

The flowers shed their leaves until the cold

Subsides and warmth again can spread to them.

Not so my coleus who tends to fold

Her lovely leaves in prayerful attitude

Beseeching me protect her cultured life.

Yet offers as her simple gratitude

The variegated colors running rife.

Aware am I that men can never rise

Once death has frozen vitals in the graves

Except the Great Creator hears their cries,

Uprooting hungry souls His coming saves.

When numbness passes through my veins with time

Replant me, Lord, in your celestial clime.

MY HEART RECALLS

When I can see the earth in spring renew
A wildly green and flowered heritage,
Then I may know depressing waste, and view
Poor bulbs that strive in dismal pasturage.
Unvalued there, the seeds are blown by wind,
The tiny roots are smothered by dull weeds,
And there some precious plants are roughly rend
By beasts or starved unless the soil serves needs.
When I perceive pale petals long for grave
While heaven snows cold flakes at freezing time,
And blossoms burst in brilliant beauties brave,
Sustained by gentle hands and strength sublime,
My heart recalls your friendship's faithful care
To nourish wilting hopes 'til life they bear.

BONN'S BEETHOVEN BOY

Small figure stands on a piano stool
Hour after hour, and what was once life's joy
To learn becomes a heavy work and rule
For Bonn's young talented Beethoven boy.

Oft lying wide awake in night-time's bed,
His fingers aching for an idle rest,
He feels the pull of Father's hands instead,
And tired, can hardly play his utmost best.

Forgetting talent, knowledge, gift and skill
He pillows piano – sleeps away fears –
Loud drunken bellows threaten then to kill
Abusive blows hurl striking, burning ears.

His mother grieving greatly all the while
Protects him in the comfort of an arm,
And holds him in the warmth of her rare smile,
Receiving with her flesh all further harm.

She senses spirit in this child is source
Of music flowing strongly through his heart,
And knows it futile to attempt to force
The destined power of a mighty art.

IF THIS BE CHRIST CRUCIFIED (WHAT THE SHROUD MEANS TO ME)

When soldiers crowned the top of His head

With a cap of thorns

Blood from puncture wounds on His scalp

Poured forth and down His face-

For me.

He stood the King.

When soldiers struck His face and broke His nose

With their fists

Bruises from their beatings

Swelled around His eyes almost blinding Him –

For me.

He suffered quietly, the King.

When soldiers scourged His back both left and right

With a leaded whip

Blood from cutting, tearing flesh

Flowed forth and toward His sides –

For me.

He bowed His head, the King.

When soldiers forced Him to lift a rough-hewn cross

Made of wood,

Abrasions formed on burden-bearing shoulders

As He stumbled under the heavy weight –

For me.

He carried the cross as King.

When soldiers nailed His wrists to a crossbeam

With a seven-inch spike

The spot of Destot enlarged to support

The body of the crucified –

For me.

He hung on the cross as King.

When soldiers nailed His overlapped feet

With a single spike

His body forced His weight downward to writhe

And breathe laboriously up and down –

For me.

He lay down His life as King.

When soldiers pierced His side

With a Roman lancia

Blood mixed with fluid which filled His chest

Burst from the gaping wound with a spurt –

For me.

He died my King.

If this image stained and scorched

Upon an ancient cloth be Him,

If this be Christ crucified;

Recorded in sacred scrolls;

Prophesied,

This mysterious man of humility is He.

He is the risen Lord.

The Soon Coming King!

ON HEARING HANDEL'S MESSIAH

My spirit sails the singing tides of tone;

Tides sweeping, surging, swelling in the air;

And so I listen- not with ear alone –

To grandeur moving soul to heights somewhere,

Compelling me to float on crest of sounds

From tender voices to compassionate string;

And sense no limitations, feel no bounds –

Majestic music glorifies the King!

I ask of You, O Lord, accept such praise

As representative of grateful hearts

Who worship You in simpler, humbler ways

Yet yearn to tell their love in lofty arts.

With oceanic beat of human drum

I pray, Messiah, let Your Kingdom come!

PART II

Short Stories From The Hills Of West Virginia

WELCOME HOME

It felt good to be home again, away from Chicago's continuous rush. Charlotte Conway was really a small-town girl at heart. She had missed this place ever since her parents moved to the windy city. Withrow, West Virginia, suited her fine with its mostly residential streets, except for its one business district where the City Hall, police and fire departments, hardware store, drugstore and clothing shop were located. If she wanted to shop at malls, go to movies, concerts or stage plays she could always drive into Huntington.

As she walked to the end of her street, she saw the familiar sign 'Dead End', and smiled. The old graveyard divided the upper and lower sections of the street. She remembered playing 'hide and seek' behind the tombstones with her childhood friends. Later, when they were teens, their favorite game was 'Spotlight'. The new cemetery lay up on a hill higher than this one and too far away for the town's children to play there. Instead of regarding their play in the graveyard as irreverent, they had enjoyed their young lives in the peacefulness of the quiet and secluded tract of land. No, their parents had not approved, but they never forbade them to play there, either.

As Charlotte strolled with her black Lab past the cemetery, her eyes spotted the dark gray stones; some of them ornate, but most of them plain. Some bearing phrases such as "Asleep in Jesus", and some with only the name, date of birth, and death.

Entering the cemetery, she headed for a waist-high wall around three graves where she and her friends would gather to talk. She picked up a couple of small water bottles and shaking her head, she smiled, throwing them in the trash barrel. Another generation was meeting in this place of repose. She sat down on the wall; and looked around at the oak trees, alive with vibrant autumn leaves and the green pine trees, once planted in love by mourners. She was older now, and the fact that there were people buried underground here came as a sobering thought to her. These were people who had lived and died, leaving loved ones to cope with grief. She suddenly realized that in all these years, she had never noticed or read the old stones. Her dog, Sadie, jumped onto the wall beside her and stood, also surveying their surroundings. She reached up and patted the animal's smooth, wide head. Sadie's brown eyes looked into her green ones; and then the dog obeyed the signal to jump down.

Charlotte walked slowly from one grave to another, reading the names, dates and phrases on the stones, wondering about each person. Something caught her attention; and she kept mentally brushing it off. After a while, though, it became obvious. The majority of death dates on the stones were the same…1927. What happened? Did a fever sweep through the community which existed then, taking its toll on the citizens? She stood at each grave, calculating their age in her mind. All ages, men, women and children had died in 1927. She could imagine the continuous funerals occurring in the various churches throughout the neighborhoods, and all the grieving families. It would mean that back then the whole town mourned. Her dog sat down, looking up at her face as she pushed her auburn hair up and back with the band she wore around her wrist.

Curious about the cause of so many deaths in one year, she reached for her cell phone stuffed in her back jean pocket and sat down, Indian-style, under an oak tree near a twelve year old girl's grave, a lone figure in blue jeans and a brown checkered shirt.

"Nineteen-twenty-seven," she read aloud. Holding the device close to her lips she spoke into it. "To Memo. Note to self. Check 1927 burials in old graveyard."

Sadie stretched out beside her.

She barely noticed a caretaker in his fifties leaning against another oak tree, a leaf blower in hand, watching her twirl a large leaf, but turned her head, instead, to stare thoughtfully at the hand carved date on the stone. 1927.

The next day, Charlotte approached the entrance to the City Hall with Sadie on a leash.

"Hey, Charlotte! Is that really you?! What are you doing back here in these parts?"

She turned around to see her long-time friend, Rick Rogers, in a police uniform, his blond hair hidden by the official cap. "Hi ya, Rick. You're a policeman now!"

"Is it that obvious?" He laughed.

"Yeah, the uniform is a dead give-away," she smiled, and he grinned broadly.

"And who is this pretty, furry lady with you?"

At the word pretty, Sadie wagged her tail and looked up at him.

"Sadie, this is Rick, a long-time friend."

On hearing the word friend, the dog sat down and offered him a paw.

"Well, aren't you something, Sadie girl." He stooped to pat the dog's head and shook the offered paw. Standing, he asked Charlotte, "Are you on vacation or just a day's visit?"

"Neither. I'm home to stay. Going to live in my parents' stone cottage on the Dead End."

Rick did an exaggerated double-take with his blue eyes. "Really!"

"Really!" She laughed. "I know we've just met up after I've been gone for a long period of time, but could I ask a favor of you?"

"Sure. Ask anything."

"Would you keep an eye on Sadie while I run into the building for a few minutes?"

"I'd love to spend a little time with this beautiful girl." Taking the leash from her in one hand, he opened the heavy glass door for her with the other as she started to enter the City Hall. "So, what do you need to do in this building?"

"Oh, trying to get a little information on the town's history."

"You mean there's something you don't know about our town? You grew up here, too, Brat."

"Just curious. Have you noticed the stones in the old cemetery?"

"Can't say that I have."

"Well, a great many of them have the same death date. I'm wondering what happened in 1927."

"In those days, the flu probably killed quite a few people, Charlotte." He suddenly grinned. "Oh…you are bored already here with us. Let's see… Bored big city investigator uncovers 'plot' to kill off small town population!"

She took a couple of steps back and closed the door. "Laugh if you want, Rick, but you should take a look at those stones. Knowing you, they will pique your curiosity, too."

"Here, let me tap my cell number into your phone, and give me a call when you get too bored. I'll show you around town!"

When he had finished adding himself as contact, she called his phone.

His eyebrows went up a notch. Looking into her face, he answered, "Hello?"

"I'm not bored yet, but now you have my number." She winked at him and entered the building.

Walking through the building and looking at the lettering on the doors, she passed the man who had been working in the cemetery the day before. He nodded to her and she smiled in his direction.

Disappointed that the record room was closed for the day, Charlotte stopped by the only floral shop in town to pick up a small bouquet of yellow flowers. A few hours later, she sat under the big oak tree with her laptop on her crisscrossed legs. Sadie lay beside her again. In front of them, the bouquet brightened the little girl's grave. The name carved into the stone was Faith.

She searched records via the Internet, finding a chart displaying the spread of influenza in the state. She learned that it didn't hit that area until nineteen-twenty-eight, and the death count didn't rise in the area until nineteen twenty-nine. She looked up from the computer, scanning the graveyard in thought.

Across the cemetery, the caretaker watched her. He leaned on the weed-eater he'd been using, wiped the sweat from his forehead with a handkerchief, and then scratched his bald head.

Charlotte was so absorbed in running down charts of diseases and setting a contact display for Rick's cell number on her phone's front screen that she didn't notice when Sadie wandered off among the stones. When she put the computer in her backpack and rose to leave, she didn't see the dog anywhere around. "Sadie!" She began calling her dog's name over and over as she walked.

She could hear a whine, and then a bark coming from the direction of a padlocked wooden shed. "What are you doing in there, Sadie?!"

Hearing her voice, the dog frantically dug a hole under the outbuilding and squeezed her body through to freedom.

Her dog dancing around her in joy, Charlotte laughed out loud. "Okay, okay, stay with me from now on, girl!"

Upon waking the next morning, she wrapped a robe around her pajamas and went into the kitchen to brew coffee and make wheat toast. Taking both out on the porch with her, she sat on the swing. She still couldn't shake her curiosity concerning the 1927 date off her mind. Sipping the last of her coffee she caught sight of a piece of notebook paper taped to one of the front posts. When she took it down, she saw penciled scrawling and made out the sentences, "If you want to know more about the people buried in 1927, meet me in the graveyard. Please leave the dog home. Dogs make me nervous."

Looking around, she asked herself, "Meet *who*? What *day*? What *time*?"

Charlotte quickly showered, dressed in jeans and a denim shirt. Pulling on socks and her brown leather walking boots, she wondered about the note. She didn't know who wrote it. Was it the caretaker? By the scrawl, surely not Rick. Nor did she know if the note meant today. Morning? Afternoon? Evening? Nevertheless, she grabbed her hobo bag and took off for the cemetery.

Feeling eyes watching as she moved among the gravestones, she stepped behind a walnut tree and waited. Standing still, she finally saw him slowly but purposefully striding from behind the old, abandoned white frame church on the lower side of the hill. His bald head and neck set at an angle above his lime colored shirt. The grin plastered on the caretaker's face suggested they were old friends who shared a secret and his pale eyes were as focused as a cat's. And they were focused on her.

"You were right," he said in a deep, even voice, still grinning.

"About what?" she asked warily.

"These people buried in 1927 didn't die from the flu, diphtheria or any sickness." His eyes narrowed.

"Oh, I never said they didn't die from a contagious disease. I was only curious why so many of the tombstones displayed the year 1927 as the date of death." She tried to make her tone of voice sound casual.

"Oh, I think you suspected something criminal. He straightened his head and shoulders and gave her a knowing look. "Anyway, I did find something that would interest you. Come with me."

A couple of crows flew overhead, cawing loudly and one landed and perched on a tombstone near her. The black-feathered creature's eyes caught her attention until, against her instincts and better judgment, she followed the caretaker.

He led her up the graveled path into the older section of the graveyard where he had parked his white truck near a grove of evergreens. Urging her to follow him around the vehicle, he motioned for her to stand beside him.

Once there, she saw an open grave. Looking at the dirt piled beside the plot, she exclaimed, "You dug up a grave?!"

"Yeah, and just like I thought, this lady's neck is broken."

"But these graves are far older than 1927." Could he, the caretaker, not realize the obvious, she wondered.

"Well, maybe she was buried in this part of the graveyard anyway," he declared. "Look closer. Just look at that neck."

She stepped closer to the grave to view a half-rotted corpse in a faded and tattered dress. It was obvious this person was buried long before 1927. The coffin, itself, was almost a mere wooden box. A pain shot through the top of her head causing her to topple into the hole and onto her side, squishing the dead body over as she landed. Shocked, disoriented and dazed, she was hardly aware when he set the old wooden coffin lid in place. Suddenly, she became aware the man was talking while he hammered nails.

"Hope I didn't hit too hard for you to hear me." He struck a nail so hard the wood nearly splintered. "You had to snoop, didn't ya? Lady, my family spent years trying to live down what my great-grandfather did. You don't know what they went through. They were disgraced and shunned. That means they lived from hand to mouth because no one would hire them. Understand?" His voice caught in anguish. "Not until people died off and time buried the past." He let out a sob. "We didn't deserve that kind of treatment. Nobody else in the family ever killed anyone. Including me, now. I'm just lettin' nature take its course. That's all. You hear me?!"

Horrified, face to face with a long-buried corpse, she calmed herself with the knowledge that the soul, the life force, the real essence of the deceased was gone, leaving an inanimate vessel behind. "Oh, God, help me!" She silently pleaded.

She remembered her phone in her back jean pocket and struggled with her free arm and hand to grab it. Apparently, the man meant to bury her phone and bag with her. She made out the contact symbol for Rick's number she had placed on the front screen and pressed down with her thumb. When she heard him answer she painfully whispered, "Help…" She heard dirt hit the coffin as some of it trickled onto her face when she tried to look up. "I need You, Lord," she begged silently again. Tears streamed down her cheeks.

Static startled her before a voice filtered through the turmoil in her mind. She could hear the caretaker's voice as he answered his truck's radiophone.

'I can't make it up to the new cemetery right now. I'm in the middle of something'. Humph. That Gary guy is a lazy no-good! This is the third time I'd have to fill in for him and help Jason dig a grave." Listening for a few minutes, he cursed. "What?! Why would I be fired?! I'm doin' *my* job! That Gary ought to be the one to go! Okay, okay, okay! I'm on my way!"

Soon, he was bellowing over her, too. "Gotta go for now, Lady, but I'll be back. Don't go anywhere!" He laughed as he slammed the door, started the engine and backed the truck out.

After he left, she mentally thanked the Lord, and tried to think what she could do to breathe better until she could figure how to get out of the grave. Her hobo bag was still draped across her body. It was difficult to maneuver her body in such a cramped position. Laying her phone on her chest, she felt inside her bag until she came across the extra McDonald's plastic straw she remembered putting in there. She used the light from her phone to locate one of the cracks where dirt had drifted inside the box. She managed to move onto her back, squishing the corpse even more, to free her other arm and hand. She concentrated on feeling the crack with her fingers and very carefully forcing the straw up past clots of dirt. Relief flooded her whole being when she breathed air instead of dust as she put her lips around the straw. Beads of perspiration from the heat inside the box mixed with the tears. Her stomach roiled with nausea as the stench overwhelmed her senses. "Now what, Lord?"

Rick was mystified and alarmed after seeing Charlotte's name pop up on his cell and answering in a jaunty tone of voice, "Hello!" All he heard, in return, was a whispered "Help…" He drove the police car to her house. Receiving no answer to his knocks yet hearing the dog barking, he went around the house to check the windows until he found the den window slightly open and removed the screen. It was a tight fit, but he wrangled his way inside. Sadie was barking loudly and wagging her tail. Rick kept dodging wet welcome licks to his face as he tried to straighten up, "Okay, girl, where is she?"

Having searched every room, he stood by the desk in the living-room, feeling frustrated. "Where did she go, Sadie?"

The dog sat on her haunches, cocking her head as if asking the same question.

It was then Rick spotted a crumpled piece of notebook paper and picked it up to read. Red flags began to wave in his head. "Hey, Sadie, come on. Let's go get her!"

The dog's front paws started prancing before she jumped up, ready to go!

Charlotte reasoned she was only prolonging her breathing until her captor came back and finished literally burying her. She knew she had to think of something to get out before he returned. "Lord, help me to think clearly and give me the strength I need. Please…" She used the flashlight on her phone to see the tips of the nails the caretaker had had time to drive into the coffin. Fishing again inside her bag her fingers finally located her pocketknife. Thanking God that the straw stayed in place, she worked one nail loose, and then another. She realized her captor only had time to shovel some dirt on one end of the coffin. With enough adrenalin and determination, she might kick part of the coffin lid off.

Entering the old graveyard, Rick stooped down to let Sadie sniff a scarf he had grabbed off the coat rack as they went out the front door. "Now, go find her, girl. Go find Charlotte!"

He tried to keep up while the dog sniffed around head stones, up a gravel path and into a grove of evergreens. He stood, looking around, when the dog disappeared into thick patches of bushes and trees. He finally stepped inside the grove of evergreens as Sadie started a high-pitched bark. "What did you find, girl?"

The dog frantically leaped around an open grave where they could see a hand sticking up from a partially removed coffin lid and attempting to push it off.

Looking at her blood-matted hair and tear-stained face, Rick lifted Charlotte out of the grave. It took some doing to get Sadie to settle down as he sat, holding the young woman close. "Who did this to you, Charlotte?"

She coughed, and then whispered, "Caretaker. He's crazy…really disturbed."

Releasing her immediately, he put his hand on his holster and looked around. "Where is he?"

"New cemetery. He'll be back."

He spoke into the radio on his shoulder, quickly explaining the situation and requesting an ambulance. In only minutes, they heard sirens wailing. After Rick called for help, he cradled her gently in his arms. "Don't worry. They're picking him up and sending help back up here." Gazing down at her, he whispered, "Welcome home, Stinker," as he softly stroked her cheek with one finger.

"Thank you, Ornery," she whispered back and weakly smiled up at him.

THE DISAPPEARANCE OF FANNY BARBERTON

"There she goes again!" Seven-year-old Hope's dark blue eyes looked up from the fudge ice-cream bar she had been unwrapping, trying not to drip any on her yellow sun suit.

We were standing in her backyard, my sleeveless pink blouse already spotted with chocolate, as I wiped fingers of one hand down my matching shorts. From our vantage point, we could see the neighbor across the alley, dressed in one of her husband's white t-shirts and khaki shorts stepping down from her back porch, yelling, "Ernie! ERNIEEE!"

Four-year-old Ernie's freckled face was red as he kept on running down the alley, perspiration beads forming beneath his light brown, close-cropped hairline, but his brown eyes sparkled with mischief as he played his favorite game.

Fanny Barberton's own face turned red as she repeatedly swung her sandy ponytail; and screamed so loudly a neighbor's chickens started to flutter, helping her out with their cackling. A few crows circled above, their cawing creating quite a cacophony in our tiny unincorporated bend-in-the-road small town of Cranston, West Virginia. Her sad brown eyes finally spilled over with tears when the two of them tired; and she grabbed him by the t-shirt, yanking him all the way home.

Hope covered her mouth with a small hand and lowered her head, letting her straight sandy-colored hair hide her face in an attempt to suppress her giggles. I stood motionless, once again my nine-year-old mind fascinated with Ernie's game and his mommy's response. Finally, I pushed my blonde bangs away from my eyes and turned toward Hope's one-floor wood-frame house, seeing our mothers' faces peering through the kitchen windows.

Hope spotted them, too. "Come on, Sheila!"

"I don't know when Fanny is going to realize the futility of chasing Ernie down the alley every day." Still wearing her blue and white striped cotton housecoat with the top of a detective paperback book sticking out of one pocket, Hope's mother, Trina Rolston, poured another cup of coffee for herself and her next-door neighbor, Amelia Fredricks, who happened to be my mother.

"How are things going with her and Burton?" my mother asked, smoothing her fifties floral, cotton dress as she sat down at the kitchen table and crossed her slender legs.

"Not so good...," Trina pushed her black hair back and gave Mother a meaningful look with her dark eyes.

Mother's eyebrows rose, and her blue eyes invited Trina to explain.

Hope and I kept our heads lowered as we ate grilled cheese sandwiches and sipped tomato soup. Yet, we were all ears, hoping our mothers thought we were too busy eating to pay attention.

Trina continued, "Peyton and I could hear them fighting all the way over here a few nights ago. Fanny borrowed coffee the next morning so early I could hardly prop my eyes open. She had a black eye, almost swollen shut. I asked her what had happened, and she said she ran into a hanger when she was searching for something in a closet." Trina rolled her eyes. "If you ask me, she probably had a lot of help running a hanger into her eye from that monster!"

Mother, who had leaned forward over the table, not batting an eyelash, nodded her auburn head before glancing at us.

We had taken as long as we dared with lunch without arousing suspicion of eavesdropping during this interesting bit of information about the neighbors across the alley.

Trina looked at us, too. "Why don't you girls go play with the toy kitchen in the basement while Amelia and I hang laundry on the line?"

Summer passed, and school started with all its events, and we were all too caught up in our own lives and Christmas in our homes to notice Fanny and Ernie's game.

When Spring brought warm days with pastel pedal pushers and sleeveless blouses for mothers and daughters, we began missing Fanny hanging up clothes or playing with Ernie. As Trina dialed her number on the telephone, Hope and I pretended to be greatly absorbed in our new books.

Burton's voice answered, and he quickly informed her, "She's not here."

"I haven't seen her in months and wanted to invite her to come have coffee and pie with Amelia and me."

"She isn't here;" he said curtly. "And she's not going to be here."

"I beg your pardon?"

"I said she won't be here anymore!"

Trina frowned. "Oh, we just became friends. If you don't mind my asking, why won't she be home anymore? Is she sick? Is there anything I could-"?

Burton cut her off. "She ran off with another man and won't be back. Now Ernie and I would like you to mind your own business!!" The phone went dead.

Trina told mother what Burton had said, word for word. Pacing the floor, she vehemently declared, "Fanny wouldn't leave Ernie with that beast! She loves her son, and I'm sure she wouldn't leave him voluntarily. Oh, Amelia, do you think he may have done something awful to her?!"

Mother's complexion paled. "I'm afraid he may have killed her."

Hope and I gasped out loud before we could control ourselves. Trina, who had apparently also feared the worst, but couldn't bring herself to put it into actual words, was too speechless to send us girls into another room.

When our daddies came home from the Chemical plant and we had all eaten supper together, the couples settled in the living room with their coffee, instructing us to go into Hope's room. We did as we were told, but since it was across from the living room we left the door cracked, and silently agreed to sit on the floor with our eyes and ears as close to the opening as space would allow.

A floor lamp and two end-table lamps illuminated the room as Trina began the discussion, telling of her telephone conversation with

Burton. She reminded Peyton of the Barberton's quarrel they had heard, going on to tell about the black eye Fanny wore when she borrowed coffee early the next day. She described the horrible feeling of fear that something dreadful had happened to her.

Mother added that they didn't think Fanny would leave her little boy, and she could be dead.

At this, both men stood up. My dad, Joe, combed his fingers through his dark waves before hooking his thumbs into the back pockets of his gray work pants. His hazel eyes stared past them all.

Hope's daddy grew red in the face, the flush spreading into his blond hairline. His green eyes narrowed, "We're going to talk to this brute right NOW!"

Mother's eyes widened. "I don't know. He's a construction worker with big muscles. He's lean and mean."

Peyton assured her, "We'll stay outside, but we have to get the truth out of him. Maybe he'll say she had an accident."

When the two men left by the back door, we slipped into the living room where we could see our mothers looking anxiously out of the kitchen windows. We scurried back to Hope's room when our daddies suddenly returned. As they moved into the living room, Mother asked anxiously, "What happened? Was there any trouble with him?"

Peyton spoke first. "He said Fanny left in a car with a man he didn't know, saying she wasn't ever coming back and-"

Trina interrupted, "What about Ernie? Did he say why she left without him?"

Joe answered, "He said she left with her bags, never looking back at the boy."

"He's lying!" Trina exclaimed.

"Couldn't we call the police?" Amelia asked.

"And tell them what, Amelia?" Joe responded. "Where's the evidence to show them and back up our suspicions? We will just have to pray the truth surfaces, and he confesses if he really has harmed Fanny."

Time passed swiftly. The events of our own lives soon took priority. The Rolstons discovered they were expecting a baby, and excitedly prepared a nursery. Mother held a baby shower for Trina at our home, inviting their women friends, all except Fanny.

Near the end of summer, Mother and Trina, lovely in their floral print dresses, walked Hope and me through the streets of our town to purchase school supplies. Happy in our matching khaki short sets reminiscent of camp, my friend and I pointed to flower arrangements brightening the neighborhoods. Chatting and laughing as we strolled back a different way, our mothers came to a sudden stop.

Trina put a hand on Mother's arm and squeezed. Our eyes followed their line of vision to Burton's white two-story frame house, the porch without chairs or pots of flowers still looking bare. The side lot next to it, however, displayed new bushes producing blossoms. An ornate birdbath graced the center; and behind it, a raised mound covered with a variety of freshly planted flowers. Gliding over the mound and perching on the birdbath, a large crow cocked his glossy-feathered black head and called out, "ERNIEEE!!"

SOUL STALKER

Eating their chicken salad sandwiches and sipping hot tea in a little diner on a Charleston street, Gina Johnson suggested to Suzanne, "Let's throw a costume party!"

Suzanne shook her strawberry blond head, "Gina, you know I don't like celebrating Halloween. Besides, I don't really care for partying with a bunch of people."

Her friend's brown eyes took on a thoughtful expression as she swept a strand of dark hair out of her line of vision. "We don't have to throw a Halloween party. It could be a…a…Fall costume party with only a few of our friends."

Suzanne's mouth worked into a wry smile as she raised her arched brows. Her blue eyes spoke for her, "What's the difference?"

"Just fun, Suzanne O'Halley," Gina urged. "We could choose a period theme, with the music, and of course, our favorite foods…and treats." As she lowered her head and looked at her friend, her eyes made an appeal.

Suzanne's mind was suddenly picking up the same signal. "Where could we throw such a party? My parents won't go for this kind of thing in their quiet, suburban home; and your sister certainly won't be in favor of you entertaining in her house."

Gina looked out the plate glass window, considering this obstacle to her suggestion. "How 'bout your grandmother's old farmhouse?"

"My grandmother is dead, and that place is in another county smack down in the middle of mountains and woods. It's been setting there vacant with all her furniture for over a year now." Suzanne shook her head again.

"It's perfect, Suzanne! You said you wanted to get away from that boyfriend of yours ever since you called off your wedding. I could paint that portrait of you for school; and you could work on your article for Journalism class. Then we could celebrate by throwing our party. We'll invite only close friends who would come all the way out there."

Suzanne considered the benefits of her friend's suggestion again as she zipped up her light beige jacket and pulled it down over the top of her brown slacks. "I am tired of the unidentified cell calls when no one says anything, and Mick's persistent calls or attempts to see me." Looking out at the busy street, Suzanne nodded her head in affirmation. "Let's go shop for our period clothes if we can find them."

"Hey, how 'bout The Sixties? I love the music from back then!" Gina's face glowed with excitement as she stood up, wrapping her short, cream-colored coat around her.

The two young women selected miniskirts at the mall, a dark blue one for Suzanne and black for Gina. Turtleneck jerseys would have to do, again black for Gina. Suzanne chose a golden one.

"Okay, Suzanne, you'll look great in those black fishnet stockings. Look, they're thigh-high, stay-up stockings."

Suzanne examined the hosiery with their open diamond shape, automatically rejecting them, then changed her mind. After all, these clothes were supposed to be a sixties-period style.

"Well, we don't want to look like twins. I'll buy the black leggings," Gina remarked.

Suzanne smiled at the thought of such two physically different women mistaken for twins. True, they could talk for hours, and in agreement, about art, literature, even politics. They both played classical music while they worked on their individual projects. Yet their difference in appearance was like comparing night and day.

While checking out, Suzanne's cell phone rang. They both paused as she checked the caller ID. "It's Mick again. He's been leaving a dozen voicemails and texts." She sighed and turned her phone off.

Two days later, Suzanne wished she had asked Gina to ride with her as she drove her silver Chevy from Kanawha into Roane County. By the time she turned onto a road between the mountains and followed a creek to a wooden bridge, she felt dread. Stopping the car, she looked across the bridge where she could see the white two-story farmhouse with its barn-shaped tin roof and big porch. The real barn loomed at a distance, weathered grey with time. She ran her perspiring hands down her jeans and pulled her green sweatshirt down nervously. Fields had grown up on either side of the house. She really didn't want to enter that house alone. Why on earth did she agree to this? Oh yes, Gina made it sound like fun. Just when did her best friend leave her part-time job at the art store, and how close was she now?

As she finally crossed the bridge and pulled onto the graveled driveway, she saw the black Honda approaching the property. Relief flooded over her whole body as she uttered Gina's name out loud.

"Hey, gal, my sister had quite a collection of mood rings. I brought one for you, and one for me. I'm wearing a green pendant instead of beads, but I knew you would wear your gold necklace with the cross. You never take it off. Guess you could wear a necklace over it."

"Jewelry, except for beads, wasn't that popular in The Sixties. My own necklace and cross will do nicely."

"Oh, Suzanne, this place is absolutely perfect for a Halloween Party," Gina exclaimed.

"I thought it was a *Fall* Party, Gina," Suzanne joked as Gina slyly smirked; and began prancing around the outside of the house in her tight jeans and blue T-shirt. Suzanne reluctantly followed her.

"Ooo, look at that carving on the stone chimney. 'Head in water.' And right there is an old well!" Gina stared in amazement.

"That's been there for years, Gina. There's no head in the well. At least I hope not."

"Well, it's ideal for a Halloween Party. Wait until the mist rolls between the mountains. I bet the woods in back there look spooky at night."

"Now Gina, we agreed to work on our assignments here, and then celebrate with a few friends."

"Oh sure…sure. You're right. I was just sayin'"

Looking at each other, they burst out laughing at their comical expressions.

The laughter eased Suzanne's nerves a little; and as they entered the house, the neatness of her grandmother's maple tables, and delicate glassware lifted her mood. She thought, "This break might not be so bad after all. Might even turn out enjoyable."

Gina brushed her fingers across a table. "Needs dusting and vacuumed, but this is surprisingly nice and cheerful, Suzanne. I wonder why your parents left the glassware and lamps and all here?"

"They're elderly; and it's enough for them to take care of their own home and expenses." Suzanne hesitated before saying, "I wasn't any help, either, always absorbed in my own interests and little world." She gazed around at the fragile objects and the floral pictures on the walls, memories filling her mind like a slideshow. Tenderness tugged at her heart.

"Oh NO! Suzanne, there's no electricity out here!" Gina kept clicking a light switch.

"Hmm…it's a good thing the temperatures are rising this week. Well…Granny has plenty of candles and oil lamps."

"Ooo…Perfect!!" exclaimed Gina.

Suzanne smiled and shook her head from side to side.

Gina ran into the kitchen to try the faucets, and yelled, "Hey, we have water! Is the gas stove working?"

Suzanne walked into the large kitchen, noticing the faded blue walls and white cabinets. She checked the stove. Feeling surprised and grateful, she informed her friend, "I guess Mom and Dad kept the water on hoping to clean the house and thought they would need to use the stove while they were here. At least we don't have to manage without these things." She picked up the box of long wooden matches from a nearby shelf and rattled them.

The next couple of days slid by quickly as they each concentrated on their assignments. Suzanne set her laptop on a small desk under the stairwell, and Gina set up an easel, paints and brushes in the kitchen.

Suzanne had brought instant coffee and creamer, tea and packets of hot chocolate. Gina contributed cereal bars and fruit for their breakfasts. The two young women bubbled over with discussions about their assignments as they opened cans of food for lunches and suppers, sometimes using canned milk with casseroles. Gina stirred up a pot of chili one night, and they curled up on the couch with steaming bowls of the thick soup. After a while, though, they both began to yearn for old fashioned hamburgers and fries; and vowed their first lunch together in town would be at a fast-food restaurant.

"I'm making home-made pizzas in your Granny's bread pans for our Hal… our celebration."

Suzanne grinned to see her friend flustered. "Donald is bringing a variety of soft drinks, and everyone seems willing to bring something. We'll be fine."

The singing of little birds, caw of crows and cries of blue jays woke them every morning as soon as dawn spread across the heavens. For an hour or so they enjoyed walking through the woods behind the house. When the sun shone, the colorful leaves shimmered. Small animals scurried across their paths, delighting them. Once, when big gray clouds rolled across the sky, it grew darker in the woods. As they slowly made their way through the trees, they heard a crack of twigs and something that sounded like footsteps. They paused, and looked at each other, then hurried to the back door.

The day before the party, Gina unveiled her full-length portrait of Suzanne.

Suzanne was amazed at how beautiful her best friend had depicted her. She had draped her subject in a long, flowing, white dress. The slender figure's arms were reaching toward a field of yellow flowers. "Gina, it's lovely. I feel honored and humble to be a subject of yours. This is the way I can only imagine myself!"

Gina's face flushed with pleasure. "I tried to capture the essence of you, not just your form. I'm pleased with it."

"I'm happy with it, too!" A smile brightened Suzanne's face.

After reading Suzanne's article on saving endangered animals, Gina declared, "Now we have reason to celebrate! Great job, dear girl!"

Suzanne felt elated, and in the mood to prepare and decorate. Gina brought pumpkins out of her car, setting some on the porch banister and some in the house.

"No Jack-o-lanterns, Gina." Suzanne reminded her. "But I do have an idea for one of the larger pumpkins." She gathered wild Autumn flowers out of the fields, hollowed out the pumpkin; and made an arrangement for the coffee-table. Gina set out candy dishes which she filled with candy corn and other sweets. They decorated the fireplace with small intertwined wildflowers, and placed candles on the mantle. They couldn't vacuum, but they swept, dusted and mopped.

Donald Cook, dressed in his navy-blue turtleneck sweater, blazer and jeans, carried a sizable cooler full of ice along with the case of soft drinks on his broad shoulders. His timid wife Sharon, wearing a blue Jackie-O dress and matching pill-box hat offered a spice cake. Doris Hall, a high school friend who had developed into a local stage actress showed off her pink baby-doll costume with round rouge spots on her cheeks, false eyelashes and cropped red hair. She was escorted by her boyfriend Wally Cranfield, a West Virginia horror film producer and director, wearing granny glasses, blue jeans and a tie-dyed T-shirt with beads. They brought a tray of various wraps to eat. Allen Lane entered next with his blond good looks, dressed in an impressive white Nehru suit. He was a local actor who attended the West Virginia State University with Suzanne and Gina. He brought Pigs in a Blanket. No one else came. Suzanne figured it was the location that discouraged others since most of their friends were from the Charleston area.

They played Sixties music on the battery-operated CD player Gina had borrowed from her sister. Monkees' songs sounded throughout the house. Suzanne actually mouthed "It's My Party and I'll Cry If I Want To"; and Wally sang along with "Hey Baby." Gina, Suzanne, Doris and Allen did the twist to Chubby Checker's "The Twist". All but Donald and Sharon played the game Twister, leading to ridiculous positions and hilarious laughter.

Donald finally lugged wood from behind the house and made a fire in the fireplace. While the fire and candlelight produced huge shadows on the walls, conversation turned to ghost stories each had heard growing up. Suzanne saw that everyone sat relaxed and engrossed in the stories but remained silent and declined when it was her turn.

"Hot chocolate, anyone? We have marshmallows." She changed the subject.

When everyone started leaving, Donald wanted to see the portrait of Suzanne. He followed Gina into the kitchen, and Suzanne hurried along, anxious to see his reaction. As Gina took the cloth off the canvas, his blue-green eyes narrowed.

"Well, what do you think?" Gina asked impatiently, worried he was mentally criticizing her work.

His fingers combed through his light brown hair. "Very creative, Gina. You've captured Suzanne's personality. This always fascinates me. It's why I love photography. There's an old Native American legend that it's possible to capture the soul in a picture."

"Isn't that how you met Suzanne…through Photography, I mean?" Gina questioned.

"Yes, I took her special high school pictures, posing her in different positions and with various backgrounds for her page in the yearbook."

"We had a good time, too, especially in the outdoor settings…and lots of interesting conversation, if I recall correctly,"

Suzanne added and smiled, remembering their first encounter which proved to lead to a good friendship.

Donald grinned. "You are correct."

All three became aware of Sharon waiting in the doorway. She lingered as Gina and Donald moved into the living-room. As Suzanne passed her, she whispered, "Be careful…don't trust anyone." She swung her long, strait honey-blond hair before pulling a hat down over her bangs and turned to leave with her husband.

Suzanne stood there, staring at her back. She knew Sharon had worked for a short time with Mick in a grocery store. Was she trying to warn her about her relationship with him? Was she implying in her own shy manner that he is dangerous?

The wind had risen, and shadows of branches repeatedly swept across the long windows; and occasionally the young women could hear scraping on the roof. They were busy picking up paper plates and plastic cups when the kitchen screen door banged making them jump. A gust of wind? They wondered. Suddenly, there was sharp knocking at the back door. They jumped again, hoping it was locked. If anyone at the party had returned for some reason, they would certainly come to the front door. Suzanne quickly, but as quietly as possible, locked it and ran softly to lock the front door. She moved slowly back into the kitchen where Gina still stood immobile with her brown eyes large with fear.

"Who is it?" Suzanne's voice sounded thinner than she would have liked.

"It's Mick, Suzanne. Let me in."

Suzanne's heartbeat quickened. "Go away, Mick!"

The old doorknob wiggled back and forth. "It's starting to storm out here, Suzanne. Please let me in."

"No! Go away or I'll call the police!"

"Don't be silly! I need to talk to you!"

Suzanne's fingers trembled as she pressed 911 on her cell. She whispered into the phone, knowing it would take a little while for authorities to reach them from the neighboring town.

"You don't understand, Suzanne. I need to discuss some things with you. Please let me in!"

They went back and forth like this for what seemed an eternity to Suzanne; and then he began banging on the door. His voice took on a desperate, commanding tone. Finally, lights from more than one police car flashed through the windows. The women could hear voices. "Step away from that door now, sir."

After a while, a police officer's deep voice asked through the door, "Can I see you a moment, Miss?"

She opened the door a crack at first, saw the officer and opened it all the way.

"Miss, it's okay now. He's gone. It's storming out here, and I'm thinking he just wanted inside. He says he's your boyfriend."

"My ex-boyfriend. He won't stop calling or coming around." Irritated, she asked, "You didn't arrest him?"

"He wasn't actually committing a crime. Just knocking on the door…but if he was disturbing you, you can rest assured he is gone. Have a good night, Miss."

"Thank you," Suzanne muttered, the banging re-playing in her mind.

She could hardly go to sleep once they had changed into PJs and t-shirts, talked worriedly over hot chocolate in the kitchen and gone to their bedrooms. Thunder shook the farmhouse; and lightning lit up the pitch-black rooms. Suzanne was grateful for the flashlights her grandmother had kept in every room.

How had Mick and she come to this? They had been very much in love and were certain they wanted to spend the rest of their lives together. His desire for them to live in Florida with his mother didn't appeal to her, though she failed to tell him. His floating from job to job, with no direction or goals when they had left high school until he trained for detective work didn't set right with her. Tears filled her eyes as she remembered how he had bowed his head when she told him she wasn't ready for marriage or commitment. Even then, she had noticed his glossy dark hair; and when he had looked up with tears in his hazel eyes, she had admired the beauty of them.

The truth is she missed him. She missed his hand on the small of her back as he guided her through a doorway. She missed his arm around her waist or shoulders as they waited in restaurant lines. She missed gazing into his eyes across a candlelit table. She missed the sweetness of his goodnight kisses. Why did he have to spoil the romance of their growing relationship by unreasonable jealous attitudes toward friends like Donald?

In time, Mick had seen her on a street, and followed her, calling her name. She kept walking with no thought of how it must hurt him. She had ducked into a diner; and took a seat in a booth. He had plopped down on the other seat facing her. "What's wrong?"

She couldn't tell him. Why didn't she? The question kept her awake most of the night. "This is ludicrous," she thought as she remembered the way he pulled the table in the booth lose from the wall, aggravating the woman who ran the restaurant. "Why am I blaming myself for his behavior? Apparently, I made the right decision. I was wrong in the way I handled the situation, but his possessiveness made it clear that he didn't want me to see Donald or take off on excursions with Gina. I couldn't have mistaken his attitude for anything but a desire to control me! Anyway, when our physical attraction would fade, what would we have in common? My only negative part in this break-up was in not explaining any of this to him…and now, it's too late," she reasoned. Her eyelids, at last, lowered in sleepiness.

Though they slept late the next morning, Gina wanted them to take one last walk in the woods since the sunshine lit up the tops of the trees. They had their usual good time catching sight of deer, rabbits and other small animals, recognizing plants, and enjoying the sound of the streams rippling over and around smooth stones.

They were in a good mood; and ready for lunch when they entered the back door to the kitchen. Gina suddenly screamed. "What…" Tears choked off her words. The cloth over her painting lay rumpled on the floor, and her portrait had a thick black X painted across the middle of it.

Suzanne didn't know what to do, and she was too shocked to say anything.

Her friend's anguish turned to fear. "They may still be in the house, Suzanne," Gina's voice lowered.

They each picked up cans of Raid spray, and stealthily tiptoed from room to room, even opening closets. It dawned on them both that the front door was partially open. They quickly locked both doors and peered out the windows. No car, no person.

Suzanne hugged her best friend. "I'm sorry, Gina. You worked so hard on the painting…and it was beautiful. I know your instructor and the students would have given you a good response."

"I planned to enter it in a contest…I could use the money…" Gina's voice trailed off. She hugged her friend again. "I still have time to do another one when I get home." Her face wore a sad expression as she said, "But each painting is always different."

As they packed their bags, Suzanne called out to Gina, "Did you notice what I did with the Fishnet stockings?"

"Can't say that I did," Gina called back.

"Oh well, it's not like I'm going to wear them again. They're not really me."

When Gina had left with a promise of having lunch together the next day, and her car drove out of sight, Suzanne settled into her own car. She turned the ignition. Nothing happened! She kept trying over and over. She reached for her cell phone and realized it was dead. She had been charging it in the car until the last night. She put both hands on the steering wheel and stared unbelievingly straight ahead. She was never so glad in her life to see Donald's red van pull up behind her.

He walked over to the driver's window. "You're ready to leave? I came to see if you two needed help in cleaning and locking up."

"I'm ready to leave, but my car isn't."

"What's wrong with it?"

"I don't know. It won't start." She turned the ignition again. Still, nothing happened.

Donald raised the hood. "Come here a minute." She stood with him staring at a wire. "It's been cut, Suzanne."

"Mick showed up last night, banging on the back door. The police made him leave."

"Well, Hon, this car isn't going anywhere until it's repaired. Don't worry, I'll take care of you."

They moved Suzanne's bags into the back of the van.

"Hate to bother you, my girl, but thought you and Gina would still be trying to straighten up the house, and I didn't stop for lunch. Do you have any food left in the house?"

"As a matter of fact, we left canned meat, and I still have some bread with me. Will that do?"

"That would do fine. Just need a little something before we set out on the road."

Suzanne smiled. "Come on in. You're my knight in shining armor. Not only was my car dead, but my cell had died also! What a predicament! The least I can do is feed you!"

"Well, I'm pleased to be of service, little lady," he impersonated John Wayne.

Suzanne laughed heartily and realized a lot of the euphoria she was experiencing was relief from feeling stranded.

Entering the kitchen, she offered to hang his blazer up on the coat rack attached to the wall. When she placed the jacket on the hook, it fell to the floor. "Oops, I'm sorry, Donald."

When she bent to pick it up a black fishnet stocking fell out of a pocket. She didn't understand what she was seeing as she rose with it in her hands. She turned slowly to question Donald.

He was standing just inside the doorway, his hands at either end of another black fishnet stocking, stretching it tightly. She searched questioningly his steady blue-green eyes. His mouth was set in a pleased and determined expression. He moved purposefully closer to her, pulling the stocking methodically over her head and around her throat.

"Oh…God…" she breathed a prayer.

In that split moment, she caught a glimpse of Mick behind Donald. Like a warrior angel dressed in denim, he raised the metal fireplace shovel high in the air with both hands. It was over so quickly she felt dazed. She watched him handcuff Donald's wrists behind his back while this supposed friend, now a dangerous stranger, sprawled on the floor.

Mick's arms surrounded her trembling body, and he assured her help was on the way. "We've been investigating Donald Cook for some time as a person of interest in several slayings of young women in various states. I'm sorry I couldn't come right out and tell you, but we couldn't take a chance on any leaks."

She nervously looked around as she heard footsteps. "Who…"

"It's okay, Suzanne. This is my partner, Tony." He nodded to a blond and blue-eyed young man also wearing jeans.

She looked from one man to another. Both were smiling reassuringly.

"Please forgive me, Mick!" She pleaded tearfully. "I'm so sorry!"

"Shh… I understand. Not knowing the situation, what else could you think, but that I had flipped out on you and become a jealous nut? I do understand. And I still love you!"

As sirens sounded closer, she lay her head on his chest, whispering, "I love you, too."

ABOUT THE POET AND AUTHOR

Photo Credit: Tommy Ong

West Virginia Poet and Storyteller, Shirley Hedrick Williams was born in Charleston, West Virginia; and spent her childhood in the Dunbar-Charleston-Cross Lanes area. She began writing short stories at the age of 11; started expressing herself in poetic forms using nature themes as analogy at the age of 15. Shirley has published poems in Journals across America through the years and received the title of A West Virginia Ambassador of Poetry as a Member of the West Virginia Poetry Society from the Secretary of State, A. James Manchin in April 1984.

Having worked in a library for 12 years, she knows what readers enjoy from a good story. Recently, she has moved her focus to write Christian Romantic Suspense novels.

Shirley is married and the mother of two grown children – a daughter and a son – both writers. She enjoys trips to scenic mountains, woodlands, and rivers with her family, but her heart will always lie in the hills of West Virginia.

Connect with Shirley at:

ShirleyHedrickWilliams@fireandgracepublishing.com

Made in the USA
Monee, IL
13 December 2024